CW00792717

Copyright © 2011 Ani Mallover Enterprises Ltd
Published in the Isle of Man by Ani Mallover Enterprises Ltd

ANI MALLOVER™ Ani Mallover Enterprises Ltd

™Ani Mallover Enterprises Ltd
MIRANDA THE POLKADOT PANDA™ Ani Mallover Enterprises Ltd

ISBN 978-0-9570875-0-7

www.ani-mallover.com

All rights reserved.
No part of this publication may be reproduced, stored in a retrieval system, or transmitted in any form or by any means, electronic, mechanical, photocopying, recording or otherwise, without the prior permission of the Ani Mallover Enterprises Ltd. All right, title and interest in and to the text, illustrations, designs, trade marks and logos contained herein are and will remain the property of Ani Mallover Enterprises Ltd and any unauthorised use or dissemination thereof will constitute an unlawful infringement of such rights which may result in civil litigation and/or criminal prosecution.

To my wonderful parents

A hundred, a thousand, a hundred thousand 'thank yous' are still not enough, you were always there for me, in the smooth and the rough! Like a sponge over the years all your love I did up soak, I happily absorbed all the words of kindness that you spoke. This is my little Panda-filled book of 'thank you', it is a polkadotty tale from me to you two.

To Babs and Gilda

Your light still warmly does glow, it lights the way of my path and shines upon me wherever I go.

To everyone that helped

You're truly marvellous and it means such a lot, your contribution is something that forget I cannot! Thank you, thank you and thank you again, I give you all 13 out of 10!

Ani Mallover™ Presents

Miranda
The Polkadot Panda

Miranda The Polkadot Panda: Enjoy each Episode of Enchantment!

Enchanting Episodes:

Tucked in a beautiful forest of
swishing, swaying bamboo,
Lived a pair of VERY happy Pandas,
such a loveable two!

Mother and cub nibbled away their days at
a leisurely Panda pace
Contented amongst the lofty mountaintops of
this faraway place.

All around them, tall trees
craned their elegant branches to the sky
Where their leaves were rustled
by the wind's gentle, rustling sigh.

The trees could have the heavens, the Pandas
were content down below,
Where upon the misty slopes, succulent bamboo
did deliciously grow.

Amanda adored her daughter, such a cuddly ball of bouncing polkadot fur
And in young Miranda's Panda life, no cause for alarm did occur!

Her days were as carefree as butterflies, fluttering by on wings of lace,
No frowns or scowls would ever be seen to crinkle her cheerful face!
She didn't walk, no! She bustled everywhere with
a joyful hoppity skip-skip,
And wasn't bothered when sometimes over her young Panda paws
she did trip.

Should it happen that she lost her stride and ended up tumbling,
with a BUMP -
She would simply get up again, without a fuss,
and merrily waggle her rump!

No trembling tears, no miserable moaning, not the slightest sign of woe,
Onwards to the next adventure, the bouncy little creature would go!

Amanda observed, with motherly amusement,
each cheery escapade,
And smiled at the mischief and merriment with which
her darling Miranda played.
Their days in dappled sunlight were spent together,
Miranda never straying out of sight
And as the pearly moon lingered above,
they huddled together each night.

Sometimes, as the stars blinked and twinkled
upon the dark velvet blanket of sky,
Amanda could not help but ponder the niggling question,
"WHY…"
Why did her sweet little cub have fur so oddly dotty?
It was certainly… unusual… for a Panda's belly to be spotty!

"However…" Amanda mused,
"To tell her may simply dampen her glee!
What if I spoil my little cub's days, so joyful and carefree
By worrying her about these cute little dots of black -
Simply because other Pandas such dark spots do lack?

It seems hardly right, scarcely fair, and a quite unnecessary act…
I think this is an instance for some loving,
motherly tact.
The dots do her no harm, they are simply a little unique,
I cannot see a good enough reason for
me of them to speak."

So Amanda did what many a wise mother bear would
And said not a word,
it would do Miranda no good.

One morning,
the sun sniffed the air
with its curious golden nose
And with a mischievous glint in its eye,
from beneath the horizon rose …

Miranda could feel the sun's warm honey rays
playfully tickling her fur
And it felt as though these golden fingertips her sense
of adventure did stir.

From somewhere inside her mother's cuddly shape
rumbled a snore and a sigh,
She was still deeply asleep,
roaming some Panda dream-place in the sky.

Just then, a dazzling, darting dragonfly zig-zagged into view,
Miranda watched as zipping above her in flashes of silver it flew!

She decided right then that simply lie there she could no more,
This bright, twinkling, diamond day she simply HAD to explore!
Taking great care not to disrupt her mother's blissful bear sleep,
Miranda snuck out from Amanda's arms with a slithering wriggle-creep…

Ah! Free at last!

She took a wonderful breath of the morning
and its crisp, sweet scent
Of flowers uncurling their petals
after a closed starlit night they'd spent.

Zizz zizz! Zig! Zizz! Buzzz! Zaggg! Zizz! Zig!
The dragonfly had returned,
its wings glinting above her head.
Zizzz zzig zzzaggggg! ZZZizzzzz!
It whizzed and away from her sped!

Chase it she would! Chase it she must!
She would run after that shining blur,
There was no way it could go
zzzzigggg-zagging too fast
for her!

Keeping her eyes
trained
above on the glittering
streak of wings,
She briskly bustled after it,
causing much grass swishings
and bamboo rustlings!

Panting a little, trying to keep up, Miranda scurried in determined pursuit.
She may not have been all that slender, but she was certainly swift of foot!

Under branches, through bushes,
between tree trunks and lush fronds of fern,
She paced after the zippity ziggity insect's each flying twist and turn.

Until, OOoomph!
With an unexpected, thumping bump,
She had a sudden collision with an odd, soft and furry lump!

Dizzy and winded and with her head in a bewildered whizz,
Miranda felt quite befuddled by her tumbling tizz!

She seemed to have landed on top of a strange, fluffy log,
When suddenly it grumbled,
"GET OFF, you rude, tubby hog!"

How very peculiar that the unidentified lump spoke!
Miranda decided to give it a curious, playful poke.
"OUCH! Get OFF! You chubby, clumsy thing!"
The fuzzy log said again, with an odd muffled grumbling.

What had caused Miranda to lose her dragonfly and come to such a roly-poly halt?
All that she knew was that it was by no means her fault!

"Ughhh! Golly!
Is there only ONE of you or did you
tackle me as a team?
You're certainly heavy enough to at least like three
elephants seem!"
Was the nasty moan that grumbled from the motionless
dark shape.

"Listen here, you horrible thing, it's because of you that my
dragonfly did escape!"
Miranda retorted, indeed she was still a trifle befuzzled,
but she'd had quite enough,
She would have no more of this sort of unflattering, cheeky stuff!

"I won't be spoken to in that nasty tone, I'll have you know!
Now get up, you nasty dark lump, your face you had better show!
I won't be insulted by a cowardly fuzzy shape of uncertain kind
You're the most awful furry lump I ever did find!"

Finally the mysterious thing wriggled free,
forming a glorious silhouette,
In a dazzling moment that Miranda would NEVER forget!

Before her stood the outline of a dark figure against the blazing sunrise,
A figure whose astonishing shape caught her by complete surprise!

It was a shape so familiar, a shape she knew so well,
And suddenly from within Miranda bubbled an excited, gleeful yell!

“Aaaaaaaahhhh YAY! Oh this is like a dream, only better - it’s true!
Hahaha! How wonderful! You’re a little Panda too!”

“Hmpph…That may be, but that by no means makes me your friend,
You thumpingly attacked me when you came hurtling around the bend.

There
I was -
cosy, content,
happily snoozing
away,
When you came and flattened
me, what an awful start to my day!

You could hardly expect me to be
friendly after a rude awakening like that,
One must never startle a sleeping Panda: that
is a well-known fact."

"Perhaps, and I'm sorry,
I didn't mean to squash you like that,
But seeing as you're quite tubby yourself,
you can hardly call ME fat!

I've never met another Panda, oh come on, friends let us be!
Please? My heart would do such a happy jiggle,
and it'll be fun, you'll see!
My name is Miranda, oh do tell me - what is yours?"
She said, and bashfully extended one of her velvety black paws.

They stood nose to nose now, Miranda could see the other
bear's eyelashes all bristly
And the soft fluffs of fur sprouting from his ears,
all tufty and wispy.
After standing like this for a just moment,
or perhaps it was a little while,
The other bear's grumpy, frowning little face uncreased into a
playful smile.

"Haha! Alright then!" He said, cheerfully shaking her paw,
"Patrick's the name,
With me around, your days will never again be the same!
Will you be able to keep up, chubby tubby Miranda,
with the pace of all of the fun?
I don't know whether you realise
what an adventure you've begun!"

And so began one of the many wonderful Panda games These cuddly little bears played since exchanging their names.

They tried to catch butterflies, they even did a little dance,
All through the forest the pair did laughingly prance!
They clambered up trees and from the branches did swing,
Miranda had never been happier, her heart seemed to sing!

But the sun was creeping quickly up higher into the sky
And so came the time for her to sadly say goodbye.

"I'm sorry Patrick, but I really had better go home
I'm not really supposed to do this naughty lonely-bear roam!
Mother will be awfully cross if she wakes up and I'm not there
And her disapproving scowl would terrify
even the very bravest bear!

Shall we meet here again tomorrow, what do you think?
It's a pity I have to go, it does like a rotten mushroom stink!"

Patrick raised his eyebrows with a smug, smirky sneer,
"Hahaha, now that's something I didn't think I'd hear!

I didn't realise you were such a timid, mommy's little bear!
Pah! If my mother worries, I frankly couldn't care!"
With his nose in the air he puffed out his chest and raised himself to his full height
Which, considering how little he was, made for an amusingly pompous sight!

"Unlike you, Miranda - I walk my own walk, I strut my own strut,
I'm no pathetic little baby bear, anything but!"

"Well," Miranda said, in a little bit
of a huff,
"You're welcome to carry on with all this
cocky, nonsense stuff,
But you're hardly a grown up, you're the same age as me
And you know very well that at home you should be!"

And so she left with a haughty waggle in her polkadotted stride.
Patrick called after her, "Wait! Plans for tomorrow!
We need to decide!"
Over her shoulder Miranda yelled, "I'll see you here, same place,
same time!"
"Alright then – hey, take a bath, you're all covered in grime!"

Came the parting words of Miranda's new little pal,
What dirt was he talking about, rude creature?
She didn't even smell!

Miranda paid him no heed and ran briskly back to her mother,
If Amanda had woken up,
She would be in quite a spot of bother!

Scampering down the path criss-crossed with the stripy shadows of bamboo,
Miranda marvelled at all that had happened since that dragonfly past her flew!

She now had a friend,
a real live bear with which to play!
No longer would there ever be an uneventful, drowsy, dreary day!

She scurried around the
last corner and her mother
came into sight.
Thank goodness!
There she was,
still soundly snoring
in the warm,
buttery sunlight!

She hadn't even noticed
that Miranda had sneakily
snuck away,
She had no idea of her
little cub's eventful start
to the day!

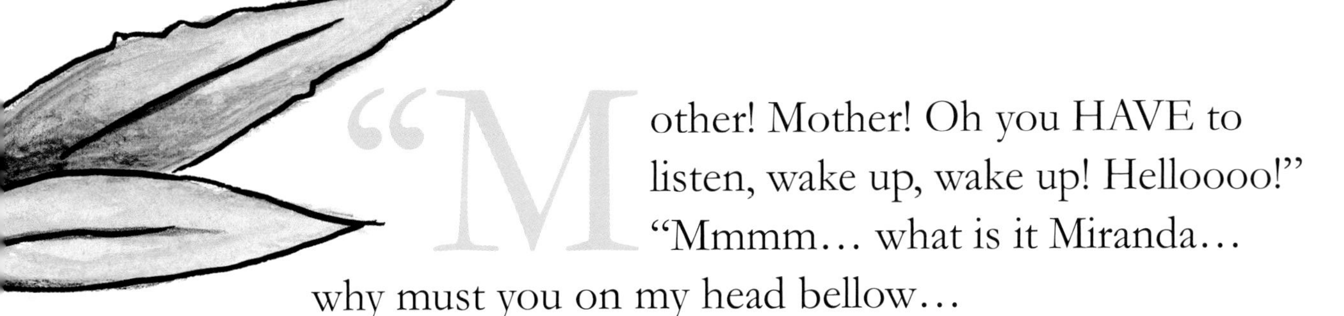

"Mother! Mother! Oh you HAVE to listen, wake up, wake up! Helloooo!"
"Mmmm… what is it Miranda…
why must you on my head bellow…
I was having the most wonderful dream about a particularly sweet bamboo shoot...
Now it is lost forever because into my ear you did so loudly hoot…"

Amanda yawned, a little grumpy, as all awakening Panda bears are.
"Oh mother, I've had the most exciting day ever BY FAR!"

And so Miranda told her all about Patrick, their games and their fun.
"But you must be careful, do not again so faraway run,
Without telling me, or otherwise your days of play will be done!"

Amanda said sternly, and gave Miranda her disapproving mother-bear stare
"But, my dear cub, I'm sure you make a lovely little pair!
I'm glad you have a friend, a partner in crime,
Just tell me before you scamper off next time."

The next morning Miranda was off for another adventurous day
Amanda waking to wave goodbye, as her little cub went on her way.

The day was crisp, luminously green and in the dawn light, daintily winking
Delicate dewdrops could be seen beautifully twinkling.

Patrick too looked forward to seeing the cheerful Miranda once more,
He had a place in particular that he wished to explore…
He was a proud little bear, perhaps a trifle too big for his paws,
a little too smug,
But beneath all this prideful pretending, he was truly as soft as a hug.

He enjoyed teasing and taunting,
but that his words caused hurt he sometimes failed to see,
For Patrick did not realise
how sensitive little girl Pandas could be!

Miranda's spots had puzzled him,
but today he would erase all doubt,
And see whether they were just patches of
dirt that could be washed out!

Miranda of course had no idea of this plan…
And with a heart light and happy towards her friend ran.

"Hello Patrick, how are you on this dazzling,
bright, delicious day?"
"Miranda, I'm wonderful, but we better be on our way!

Come, follow me, let's be off, let's go, go, GO!
There's a fantastical place that I must to you show!"

So they scampered along, two bustling bundles of excitable fur
Miranda dashed in pursuit as Patrick gambolled in front of her.

Two blurs of black and white, bounding through the bamboo
That all around them with lush tall stalks voluptuously grew.

"We're here,
we're here!
Ah, Miranda!
Come on, you
plodding Panda,
I want you to see!
Come stand beside me here, beneath this
low branch of the tree!"

A glorious pink Chinese Toon tree
waved to Miranda with its
rosy-leafed branches,
Whilst beneath
it was a cross
Patrick,
impatiently
sitting on his
haunches.

"I'm coming!
I'm coming!
There was a flower on the way I had to stop and smell!
No need to be so bossy! No need for that angry tone in your yell!"

Miranda said with a
panting puff,
The silly Patrick,
so quick to be in a huff!

She arrived by his side,
and what a gloriously serene
sight she saw,
But before she knew
what happened,
Patrick gave her a shove
with his paw!

SPLASH! He pushed her into the glorious pink pond!
All a-splutter,
"HOW DARE YOU?"
with a gurgling rage Miranda managed to utter!

The tranquil watermelon coloured pond of
just a moment before
Was now the scene of an almighty,
rippling roar!

Patrick had also jumped into the pond
and at a dizzying, swirling pace,
round and round in circles
the poor Miranda he did chase!

"Oh! You're mean! It's cold!
Now my fur's all wet!"

"Well, to take a bath yesterday,
clearly you did forget!"
Said Patrick, and splashed her all the
more.

Until, exhausted,
for his mercy Miranda did implore!
"Stop! Stop!
I'm getting dizzy!
For all this spiralling
swimming I was not
made!
I'm a Panda that safe and
dry on the land should have
stayed!"

She squirmed out of Patrick's reach before further into the pond she did sink
And stretched herself out beneath a lazily fluttering branch of pink.

Miranda shut her eyes, mmmm, this was much better!
Than there in that pond where it was colder and wetter!

Here beneath this lovely tree, with leaves the colour of grapes and strawberries ripe,
Miranda decided she was definitely the land-mammal type.

She could hear the odd splishing splash from Patrick… the occasional shout…
Aaahh… a nice little nap would be WONDERFUL, of this she had no doubt…

Miranda ignored Patrick's taunting and dozed off,
soft slanting sunlight drying her fur…
Until she awoke with a start – something was prodding her!

It was Patrick – really, he could be most annoyingly irritating at times!
Had he not told her himself that to wake a Panda was the most
serious of crimes?!

"Hey! What's this! These spots on your belly!
I thought it was because you were a little dirty and smelly!
But we've been in the pond, that should have washed them away,
Golly, you're an odd Panda, I do have to say!"

Miranda looked at him, still dozy, and with eyes batting a drowsy blink,
She said, "Hmmmm? Are you mad? I'm not dirty and I certainly don't stink!"
"But see here, on your fur, you have these oddly shaped spots,
Goodness me - they're black furry polkadots!"

Miranda was puzzled,
what was the pestering, plump Patrick on about?
So she had a few spots, wasn't that normal,
was there a need for him to shout?

"Miranda, come with me and see for yourself, this is no joke!
I am not merely at you trying to fun poke!
Come with me to the water's edge, and tell me what you see
A strange spotty you, and a nice white-bellied me!"

With a sigh and a frown Miranda decided to give up her napful rest,
Really, Patrick her patience did test!

They stood with their paws in
the gooey, chocolatey mud,
And for some reason Miranda's
heart began nervously to thud…

There, floating before them, a glinting,
shimmying reflection she saw!
Patrick pointed at it with a triumphant
waggle of his paw:

"Ha! You see! Look at those ugly black dots!
You should be worried Miranda, you should be worried lots!
Pandas ought to have shiny white fur on their tummy's,
sparkly and pure -
Certainly not covered in murky black splotches like your
polkadot fur!

You may never have met other Pandas,
but I've known quite a few
And never have I met one with spots – until you!"

Miranda peered into the sneering still pond,
what a watery tattle-tale,
Showing Miranda's belly
all spotty, and Patrick's… pale!

Could it be? Was it true? Oh what did it mean,
what should she do?!

"Hmph, Miranda, calling yourself a Panda, you impostor you!
All I know is that real Pandas don't have spots,
and it is clear to see,
That you have one… two… WAIT!
You have far more than three!
Can you explain this, can you tell me why you told such a lie,
Because if you're truly a Panda, I'll bake you a bamboo pie!"

"I…I…I… don't… I don't know what to say…"
Miranda's voice trembled with forlorn, down-hearted dismay,
"I… I eat bamboo, I have black eyes… I am a Panda…
Of this I am quite sure…
But I never knew there was anything wrong…
Oh I wonder, is there a cure?"

"Well your mother must be terribly worried,
to have a cub like you!
I wonder whether to send you away one day was
what she planned to do!
I mean,
it must have upset her to have a
daughter so spotty,
There's simply no hope for a Panda
all polkadotty!

In fact, I'm not sure we can still be
friends,
I don't know what my mother would say
If she heard that with such an odd,
pretend-Panda I had spent my day!"

Patrick said these last words
with barely the trace of a joke.
Miranda was unsure whether he teased,
or whether he earnestly spoke.

One thing was certain, he was right, her belly did have spots…
But what could she do about these un-washable,
pond-defying polkadots?

"Oh Patrick! Don't say that! That's beastly and ghastly!
Cruel and unkind and just nasty!"

"Miranda, it is quite simple, don't you see?
Before we were just two Panda's, but now there's a you and a me.

A ME," he jabbed a paw at the rippling pond,
"With white tummy fur,"
"And a YOU, with strange polkadots!" he said,
pointing to the reflection of her.

"You're strange, you're unusual, there is something not quite right,
About a Panda with polkadots, this is not a normal sight!

Haha, I have a joke, what has no friends and is covered in spots?
An odd, ugly Panda with strange polkadots!"

While Patrick chortled at his mean,
unkind, unfunny joke,
Miranda with a quiet, sorrowful shiver
in her voice spoke.

“I see Patrick. Yes, I see quite well.
No need to laugh. I’m going, farewell.”

Patrick, the cruel creature,
was so busy chuckling he did not even see -
That with a dreadfully despondent dismay,
Miranda away did flee…

Poor little Miranda
tumbled and stumbled,
Scampered and bumbled,

Poor little bear, running as fast as she could -
With polkadots and all, runaway, she would!

The trees swished and shuddered their leafy
blossoms in alarm,
As this small black and white blur rustled
through the calm.

She ran and ran as fast as her paws could go,
Over cold mountains tall and through
lush valleys low!

Up hills, through streams, to who knows where,
Went the hurrying and scurrying,
sorrowful little bear...

Until – run, run, run she could no more.
Her legs were wobbly and weak, her heart still sore.

And now from the melancholy clouds brooding in the sky
Sad raindrops fell in a watery, woeful sigh.

Her fur was soaked through and through,
What was poor little Miranda to do?

Beneath the trembling teardrops of rain splattering from the trees,
She curled into a bewildered ball, hugging her knees.

“I’m far from home, far from mother, oh how far I have ran
I can scarcely remember from where I began!”

How do you go back to the start if you don’t know where you’ve ended?
Why did she think that by running, her spirits would’ve mended?!

Now she was lost, alone, a shivering, spotty, forlorn fuzz.
Oh the silly things that a broken-hearted bear does!

"Oh I hate my spots! These silly dots!
They've gotten me into trouble, lots!
I just want to be an ordinary little bear,
Without a worry, without a care!

I want to chase the butterflies, I want to smell the flowers!
I want my days to be bursting with happy, cheerful hours!

Now that I know that normal I'll never be,
How can my heart ever be filled with glee?

I'm strange, I'm odd,
I have spots that should not be there!
Oh I am a terrible excuse for a Panda Bear!

No one will ever want to be my friend…
I shall be a lonely bear to the very end!"

Miranda sobbed, her eyes brimming with plump salty tears,
…When an odd flapping noise greeted her ears!

Puzzled, she looked up at
the droopy branches above her head.
"Wellllllllll heeelllooo there, my name is Fred!

It is actually Godfrey Frederick the Golden Pheasant –
but goodness - what a jumble!
It is such a lumpy, tongue-twizzling fumble-mumble!"

Never before had her eyes beheld such a sight,
It was such a feathery explosion of colour, that it gave her a fright!

"Well hellooooooo there!" the talking rainbow cooed again,
with a sly wink,
"You're an adorable, little bear, don't you think!"

"No I'm not! You're a liar! Oh do go away!
I've had a most dreadful, disastrous, dismal day!
I ran so very far just to be alone,
Won't you please go back to wherever it is
from where you've flown?"

A strange chortling sound chuckled from the bird
He really was most unusual-looking, truly absurd!

A vivid red burst from his chest,
Upon his head sprung a dazzling yellow crest,
His neck shone a brilliant orange, striped with black,
But what a patchwork quilt was this odd fowl's back!
Shimmering turquoise, dark ocean blue,
A splash of red, a swish of gold too!

A tail erupted in a flourish of colours so bright
Miranda was certain it would glow in the dark of night!

What a magical creature, perhaps it was a dream,
He was too fantastically feathered to truly real seem!

"Have you been sitting up there the whole time?"
"That I have, and you can certainly put up a good whine!"

"Oh go away you nasty rainbow of feather,
I'm feeling as downcast and dreary as this weather!
All I want is to be left alone and in peace,
Me and my awful spotty fleece!
And anyway what do YOU know about being dotty
when one should be plain;
About being so odd-looking you'll never have friends again?"

Miranda retorted to the intruder with a tearful frown,
Who did he think he was, this half-bird, half-clown?

"Ha-ha-cha-cha-ha-cha-cha-cha!
What a feather-ticklingly-funny creature you are!
Let me tell you a joke! Will that make you less sad?
A good joke giggle always jiggles out the bad!

What is quite round, black, white and a little blue?
A silly sad Panda! That's YOU!
Cha-hahaha-cha-cha-haha!" Fred chortled with glee,
Shuddering and shaking all the raindrops from the tree.

They flickered to the ground in flashing silver drops
And landed on Miranda with splattering plops.

"Stop that! Stop it at once!
I'm already soaking wet!
I didn't come here to be laughed at,
I came here to forget!
You're a horrible, strange looking bird, why should I listen to you,
When it looks as if into seven pots of paint you flew?"

Just as Miranda gave herself a hearty shake,
The branch above her made a shivering quake.

Suddenly, the leaves rustled, and there was a swift,
swooping whoosh of air,
As Fred gracefully flew from his perch to sit beside the bear.
He looked up at Miranda, his face wizened with concern,
"Now you listen little bear,
there is an important lesson you must learn.

I didn't mean to ruffle your fur by laughing
when you were sad,
I am no mean-hearted bully of a bird, I'm just a little MAD!
What you said was mean, and what you said was unkind,
But for the moment, we'll leave all that behind."

Fred shuffled a little closer and extended a wing,
A bedazzling, shimmering, jewel coloured thing.
He placed it tenderly around Miranda's hunched shoulder,
And now she could see he was no young bird, rather older.

As little patches of sunlight blinked through the trees,
Earnestly, Fred said, "Now, allow me, if you please,
To tell you something important,
something you must never forget,
Even if it is told to you by the strangest bird you've ever met.
Little bear, laugh at yourself you must,
If you are to go through life frown-free and unfussed!

If you can't admit to the silly things you do
and burst out in a giggle
Then you will squiggle your thought-thinker
into a terrible wiggle!
You will always be offended, you will always be discontent,
When a little humour at your expense is spent.

Now, look at me,
I'm quite a fantastically
odd-looking fellow,
What with my splashes of red, my flashes of yellow!

Do you think I have not been the subject of many a joke?
Do you think others do not constantly at me fun poke?
Insults! Ha! I've heard them all!
And when I was a scruffy young chick how they made me bawl!

Fortunately I have a beak, not a nose that could be put out of joint,
Every time that someone at me would cruelly laugh and point!
But you see little bear, this is who I am, this is ME -
I'm the me-est ME that there ever will be!

So, yes, I look like I collided with a rainbow,
I am multi-coloured from golden head to orange toe,
Who cares that I am a flying one-bird-freakshow!
I tell you what I do, I plump out my chest!
I waggle my golden banana coloured crest,
Because at being ME -
I want to be the BEST!"

Miranda sat and listened,
saw the glint in Fred's eye…
Perhaps he was right that
of her spots she ought
not to be shy.

Before she could interrupt,
he fluffed himself up just a tad,
In the company of such a
fantastic creature,
she forgot that she was sad!

Fred continued, his voice warm and mellow,
"So that is why, little bear, you have amused me so!
You and all your moaning, groaning, tears of woe!

'Poor me, I have spots, my life is doomed to gloom!
Poor me, for happiness in my heart I no longer have room!'

Aah you silly little bundle of black and white fluff,
That is truly RIDICULOUS stuff!
You are not your nose or your eyes, your tail or your paws
You are YOU - just because!

Who cares about your outside layer, spotted or not,
It's what is inside you that matters - a lot!

Now come with me, and look at this puddle,
It will clear up all that silly
Panda-mind-muddle!"

Fred hopped towards a little pool twinkling in the dappled forest light,
Miranda ambled with him,
to stubbornly say no, did simply not seem right.

There, Fred peered into the puddle,
looked at her and said,

"See there! A spotty Panda,
and her friend, Fred!
I am by far the more
ridiculous-looking of us two,
But wait,
I have something special
to show you!"

Fred dipped his wing into the water, how it rippled and shone -
And into tiny little waves, the picture of them was gone!

"You see – who you are on the outside, reflected here,
Can be poked and prodded, it can even disappear!

But who you are on the inside, the part where you are the you-est YOU,
That is always with you, and to that YOU part you must be true!
That is what you must find out, little bear, who lives inside you there
Because whatever fur she's covered in, it's about her that you should care!

So what if there's something a little strange about your spots?
I say FLAUNT your polkadots!
It makes you different,
it makes you YOU –
And to be the very best
YOU is all that
you can do!"

Miranda wanted to believe him,
believe that spotty was alright…
Perhaps there was no good reason for her to have
scampered off in fright.

And yet… wasn't it true that she would never normal be?
That the 'oddly dotty Panda' was all anyone would ever see?

So with a sigh,
her warm chocolate eyes filled with melting sadness,
She could not yet take to heart her winged-friend's
gladness.

"But Fred, I only had one friend, Patrick was his name
And he said that because of my spots we would
never be the same.
He said I was different, odd, a mistake of a bear."

"But my dear Panda, that makes you rare!
Look at you, with your delightful dark sprouts of hair!
I bet you Patrick was jealous, I bet you Patrick was sad
That he no playful polkadots of his own had!

Now, listen to old Fred, rainbow feathers and all,
No more slouching, pull up your shoulders tall!
Nose up, chin out, tail all-a-twitch,
You go show that nasty Patrick snooty-snitch!

A snooty-snitch is the worst type of friend you could find,
They say nigglingly mean things and are terribly unkind!
Usually it is because they think they're better than you,
But that, little Panda, is simply not true!

They are them, you are you, and I am just me,
There is no good or better or best between us three!
So, go waggle your polkadots right under that snooty-snitch's nose
And see how with grasshopper-green envy he glows!"

Miranda looked into Fred's shimmering pale eyes,
They sparkled with the translucent blue of early summer skies.

"You're right Fred! By golly you are!
I have been an awfully cowardly bear so far!

I thought that by running away,
I could leave my spots behind,
Yet by the time my paws could take me
scampering no more,
what I did find?
That my dots were still with me,
my troubles still here,
That by running and running my woes
would not disappear.

Hah! That nasty Patrick, what is it you
called him, a snitchy-snoot?
I'll go tell him that he's horrible and that I
don't give a hoot –
Who cares what he calls me, how he laughs,
what he says, what he does…
I am starting to like my strange spotty fuzz!

I'll tell him straight, I'll tell him right there,
That he's a nasty, pudgy,
preposterous Panda bear!"

Miranda stamped a purposeful paw and stuck her
nose in the air!

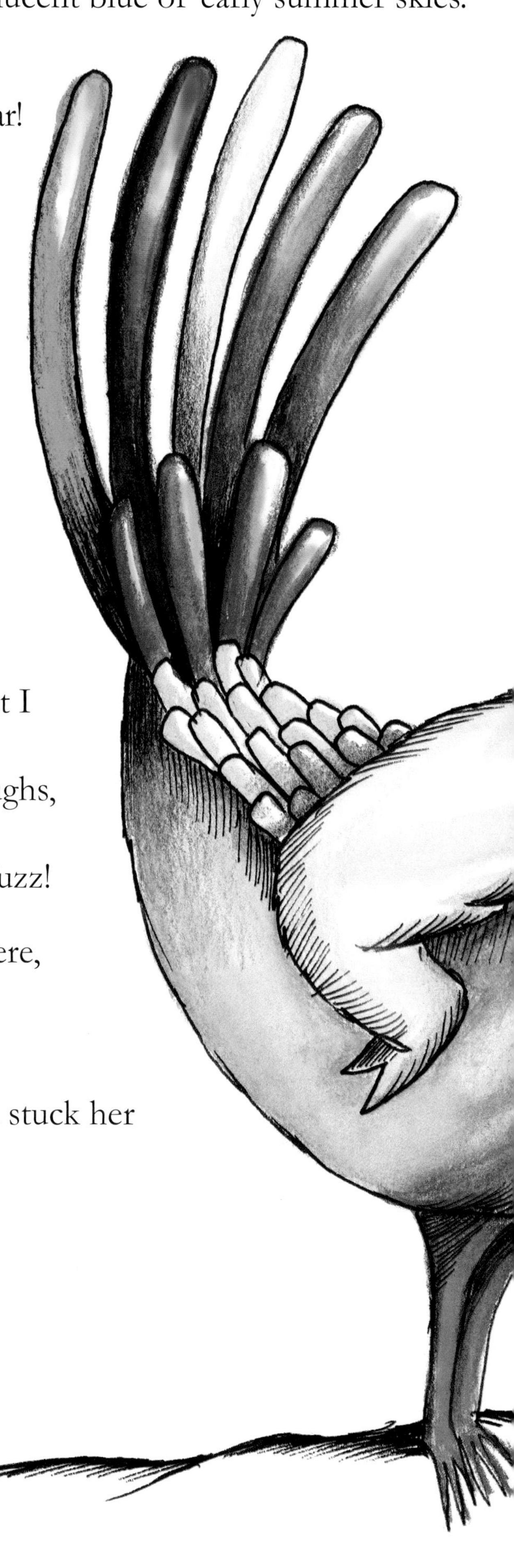

"Hmmmm...." Fred murmured,
his feathery eyebrows clustered in a frown,
"Hmmmmm…Little bear, it is best that you calm down.

Cha-ha-ha-ha, you youngsters! Always ready for a fight!
That is the way to make your heart heavy, and we want to keep it light!

I actually called your friend Patrick not a snitchy-snoot but a snooty-snitch
But that is not the problem with your plan,
that is not the glitch!

Yes, yes, I want you to be proud of who you are,
To prance happily in your pretty polkadot coat,
both near and far!

However, I'm worried that I have been misunderstood
To go and say those things to Patrick will
do you no good!

Now, I know I am just an odd-looking, colourful feathery firework,
But believe you me – don't let huffy-puffy, angry scowls on your Panda face lurk!

Remember this, remember what I say:
to hold onto a grudge,
Is to fill your insides with a slimy, oozy, ugly sludge!

If you keep all that unforgivingness rumbling within you,
It will bubble and goo and simmer and brew,
Until you overflow with that horrible, smelly, sticky, nasty stew!"

The clouds had started to drift
off into faraway corners of the sky
And dripping through the leaves,
puddles of sunlight came at their feet to lie.

Miranda looked at Fred, her nose crinkled and puzzled -
It was fair to say that her thoughts were altogether confuzzled!
Hadn't he told her that what Patrick had said was wrong?
Hadn't he encouraged her to be strong?

"Oh you dear bird! You are talking gibberish,
a strange load of twaddle!
And you have put my little bear brain into a terrible wobble!
So I oughtn't to be angry at Patrick, for all the mean things he said?
You are going to have to explain yourself, dear Mr. Fred!"

Miranda said playfully, wiggling one of her fluffy black ears,
One would never have guessed that she had only just been in tears!

"Cha-cha-cha-ha-ha-ha oh you naughty little bear!
Very well, the method behind my madness with you I will share.
Nothing gives snooty-snitches more smugly, grinning delight
Than to see that they have tickled your nostrils and made you fight!

That's what they want - they want to win, to see that you're upset,
That's no way to show them you're worthy of respect!

If you greet them with a cheery, unconcerned little wave
They quite simply do not know how to behave!

And by forgiving them,
by letting your grizzly, grumpy anger gloom go
You'll feel whiter and lighter than the flakiest flake of snow!"

Then, Fred did an unexpected thing - an odd tail-waggling dance!
Jiggling and wiggling and zig-zagging in a
hopping hoppity prance!

Miranda's eyes grew large as she took in this most odd sight,
Occurring in the forest's shadowy, leafy, lustrous light.

Had Fred finally lost his marbles, lost the plot, gone off his trolley?
Or was he simply being exceedingly, joyfully jolly?

Seemingly reading her thoughts, the jitterbugging bird chortled,
"Cha-ha-ha-ha-ha I've not gone even more mad, never you fear –
I'm simply trying to rustle you up a special souvenir!"

At last, a single tail feather fell silently upon the ground –
A dazzling spear of warm gold, the most beautiful to be found!

Fred was positively bristling by now, his feathers all a-fluff,
"Come little Panda, it is time for you to be tough!
No more dithering! No more dallying! Enough, enough, enough!

Take this feather with you, it will bring you lots of luck,
It will remind you to be kind, it will encourage you to have pluck,
And if you ever should miss me, if ever you feel alone,
Look at the sky above you, and you'll see where I have flown."

Miranda wasn't certain precisely
what he meant, did not know quite
what he did say,
But she was filled with a certain sense of sadness,
a lingering dismay…

"So, is this goodbye, are you telling me to go?
Oh but Fred, you're the loveliest friend!
Come with me! Don't say no!"

"Little bear, it is time that you are brave,
and your mother will be worried.
It is time that swiftly homewards your
little polkadots hurried.

You'll find the way if you listen to your heart,
It is the truest part of you, the thing that sets you apart.

It will tell you where to go, it will help you along the way
And you'll always see me streak across the heavens
on a sunny rainy day!"

With that, Fred picked
up the shimmering,
glinting, feather of gold
and as he warmly spoke,
he held it out for Miranda to hold.

"Now, of sad goodbyes I will frankly hear no word.
You've had enough of the ramblings of this razzdazzling coloured bird!
You must take your polkadots, you must take this feathery gift,
If you ever feel down in the grumpy dumps, it will give your spirits a lift!

Go little Panda, with your dashing dots,
Go and leave me to fly into more paint pots!"

He gave her a friendly little tap on the rear,
And suddenly she felt no sorrow, felt no flutterings of fear.
She wanted to do him proud, this oddly feathered fowl,
Who had, with his words of wisdom, chased away her scowl.

"Goodbye Fred."
With only a small, teary tremor she said.
"I will never forget you,
you funny looking bird,
I will never forget the things from you
that I was so lucky to have heard.

Look after yourself, take care,
My name is Miranda, the Polkadot Panda Bear."

She bent down,
gave him a little kiss on the cheek,
Perhaps a small teardrop from
the old bird's eye did sneak...

Miranda picked up the gorgeous
golden plume
As late afternoon drowsily darkened,
and dusk began closer to loom.

"I better go,
I don't want it to be too dark on my way,
All I have left, is 'thank you', to say."

The glinting golden feather in her
paw she carefully did place,
But in a flickering blink,
Fred disappeared without a trace!

Where had he gone?
There was no sound, no flutter, no flap!
He really was a puzzling,
brain-fuzzling chap!

Slightly perplexed, and a little upset,
Miranda fluffed out her fur –
Was THIS to be his goodbye to her?

Hmmph, anyway,
she had better be on her paws,
better be gone,
Her road home was uncertain,
she needed to leave while the sun shone.

Trundling out from the forest and it's
whispering, dripping, curious leaves
She saw a SIGHT – a spectacle that
caused her Panda heart to heave!

Miranda laughed, a ridiculous,
happy Panda chuckling guffaw
That rumbled from the tip of her ears
down into each fluffy paw!

Could it be? Could it be?
Could this be her friend?
Here to help her to the very end?

Stretched across the sky
in a big, colourful upside-down smile,
Was a dazzling, glittering,
shimmering RAINBOW that grinned over many a mile!

She would follow the rainbow, chase down its tail,
It was certain to lead her straight home, without fail!

There was a lightness in her paws,
a cheerful skip in her stride,

Miranda dashed all the way home,
a streak of joyful polkadot Panda pride!

THE END

Panda Facts:

Important things to know about Miranda and other Pandas and why they need YOU as a friend

Except for Miranda, **Pandas don't usually have polkadots.** Their proper name is the **Giant Panda,** and like our little Miranda, they are friendly, cuddly animals that live in the green, **misty mountaintops of China.**

Patrick's fluffy, chubby shape is typical of Pandas. These **hungry bears** spend most of their time happily **munching on bamboo** and can eat as much as **38kg (84 pounds)** of their favourite crispy green snack a day! That would be like you tucking into about **254 apples every day!**

Some **silly people** suggested that Pandas weren't really bears and that they **belonged to the raccoon family,** but luckily they have been put in their place and **everybody agrees** that Pandas are **definitely proper bears.** They do make **strange noises** though, not like their other bear cousins - in fact, they **squeal and bleat** like strange sheep! But that doesn't matter – we still love them!

When Miranda was **born,** she was a lovely **rosy pink colour** - just a tiny, squidgy little thing the size of a **small squirrel,** about **900 times smaller than her mommy Amanda,** but soon she would grow into the fluffy, cuddly little bear that we know, big enough to get up to all her adorable mischief!

The **horrible thing** is that Miranda, Amanda and Patrick are in more than a bit of **trouble**, because us **naughty humans** are busy **destroying** their nice green **bamboo forests.**

The more of their leafy living space that we chop down, the **less the Pandas have to eat** and the **smaller the area they have to roam around in**. We wouldn't like it if Pandas came and ate all the yummy food in our kitchens and decided to boot us out of our human houses, but that's exactly what we are busy doing to them, and **it is making them very sad!**

And it's not just Miranda and her Panda friends we have to worry about, because they **share their forests** with lots of other amazing creatures that are all being squeezed into tinier and tinier spaces and **won't be able to survive** if it carries on like this. There are **only about 1600 Pandas left** in the whole world and they are all getting a little bit worried that if us humans carry on with our silliness, there won't be any Panda's left in a few years - and that would be awful!

Miranda wants us to help her and her Panda friends by making sure that they will have **enough food and space to grow up** to be big Pandas, with little baby Panda bears of their own one day! But if us **naughty people** keep **chopping down** the Panda snack supply, those babies are going to be hungry, and **won't be able to survive. A world without lovely Pandas – what an awful thought!**

So it is **time that we look after our cuddly Panda friends,** and show them that we want to protect them and their lovely forest home. If we don't stop our selfish nonsense soon, these **beautiful bears will disappear forever** – all that will be left is pictures in a story! We want our Panda friends to keep nibbling away for many, many, many years to come, but **we need to give them a helping paw** today, if we want them to still be there tomorrow.

Go and visit **www.ani-mallover.com** for **lots of clever plans to be a Panda friend,** and see what you can do to save these beautiful lovers of bamboo!

"Who is Ani Mallover?"

With intrigue you may ask,
Yet answering that question is no simple task!
Part magician, part storyteller, part fable, part fact,
Part teacher, part friend, part truth, part act!
Don't even try to pin her down, puzzle her out or put her in her box,
She is filled with mystery,
from the top of her hat down to each of her socks!

It is said that while we are sleeping, safe and at home
Her elusive, shimmering shadow the moonlit evening does roam.
With her faithful butterfly, Fifi, always a-flutter by her side,
With her pens, and her book, she sets out far and wide
In search of a new, delightfully dazzling story
About some wonderful creature and its life most extraordinary!

For you see, all the animals do love Ani so,
And follow her about wherever her nimble feet go.
She is able to hear them, their creature-speak to understand
And has promised that she will tell their tales and so lend a hand
To make sure that everyone – young and wrinkled, near and far,
Will hear their stories and see how truly splendid they are!
For sadly the animal voices fall deaf on so many an ear,
And there are many lovely creatures who for their future do fear.
Which is why Ani with her stories has come to enchant,
She is here to speak on behalf of her furry friends who can't!

There is not much about this elusive lady that we do know,
We cannot say from where she comes or predict where she will go!
But should you ever lie awake in the inky mystery of the night,
Remember to listen, for there is a slight chance that you might
Hear the swish of Ani's cloak, see a glimpse of her hat
Hear her footseps quickly passing with a rat-a-tat-tat!
For when the night is still, the stars asleep and the moon's pearly face aglow with a smile,
You may know Ani Mallover is out there, somewhere, chasing stories over many a mile!